The Doorbell Rang
by Pat Hutchins

Greenwillow Books, New York

P9-CMO-485

The full-color paintings were done in ink and watercolor. The typeface is ITC Zapf International.

The Doorbell Rang. Copyright © 1986 by Pat Hutchins. All rights reserved.

Printed in the United States of America.

For information address HarperCollins Children's

Books, a division of HarperCollins Publishers,

10 East 53rd Street, New York, NY 10022.

www.harperchildrens.com

First Edition   13 LP 20

For Jack and Charles

Library of Congress Cataloging-in-Publication Data

Hutchins, Pat, (date)   The doorbell rang.
"Greenwillow Books."
Summary: Each time the doorbell rings, there are more people who have
come to share Ma's wonderful cookies.   [1. Cookies-Fiction]   I. Title.
PZ7.H96165Do   1986   [E]   85-12615   ISBN 0-688-05251-7
ISBN 0-688-05252-5 (lib. bdg.)   ISBN 0-688-09234-9 (paper)

"I've made some cookies for tea," said Ma.
"Good," said Victoria and Sam. "We're starving."
"Share them between yourselves," said Ma.
"I made plenty."

"That's six each," said Sam and Victoria.
"They look as good as Grandma's," said Victoria.
"They smell as good as Grandma's," said Sam.

"No one makes cookies like Grandma,"
said Ma as the doorbell rang.

It was Tom and Hannah from next door.
"Come in," said Ma.
"You can share the cookies."

"That's three each," said Sam and Victoria.
"They smell as good as your Grandma's," said Tom.
"And look as good," said Hannah.

"No one makes cookies like Grandma,"
said Ma as the doorbell rang.

It was Peter and his little brother.
"Come in," said Ma.
"You can share the cookies."

"That's two each," said Victoria and Sam.
"They look as good as your Grandma's,"
said Peter. "And smell as good."

"Nobody makes cookies like Grandma,"
said Ma as the doorbell rang.

It was Joy and Simon
with their four cousins.

"Come in," said Ma.
"You can share the cookies."

"That's one each," said Sam and Victoria.
"They smell as good as your Grandma's," said Joy.
"And look as good," said Simon.

"No one makes cookies like Grandma,"
said Ma as the doorbell rang.

and rang.

"Oh dear," said Ma as the children stared
at the cookies on their plates.

"Perhaps you'd better eat them before
  we open the door."
"We'll wait," said Sam.

It was Grandma with an enormous
tray of cookies.

"How nice to have so many friends
to share them with," said Grandma.
"It's a good thing I made a lot!"

"And no one makes cookies like Grandma,"
said Ma as the doorbell rang.